STEEPLEJACKS IN BABEL

TURNER CASSITY

Steeplejacks
in
Babel

 DAVID R. GODINE

David R. Godine   Publisher
Boston, Massachusetts
LCC 73-76687
ISBN 0-87923-070-3

The following poems were originally published in *Poetry*: The Condemned of Belgrano, Eva Beatified, Pacelli and the Ethiop, A Ballade for Mr. Rhodes, DeLesseps Go Home, Vultures over Ancon Hill (under the title Mascots), Plot for a Guianese Operetta, The Shropshire Lad in Limehouse, By the Waters of Lexington Avenue, What the Sirens Sang, Cartography is an Inexact Science. The following appeared in *The Southern Review*: Manchuria 1931, A Crown for the Kingfish, The Last of Vichy, Tonio in Mogador. Where the Cross Is Made, Two Hymns, and The Prisoner's Variety appeared in *Counter/Measures*. The *New American Review* originally published In Sydney by the Bridge and Terry Meets the Lusiads. *Emory University Quarterly* published Carpenters and Drinking Song for Tired Jaycees. The Entrance of Winifred into Valhalla was originally published in *Quince*. L'Aigle A Deux Jambes and Blood and Flatiron appeared in *Poem*. *Foxfire* was the original appearance of Making Blackberry Jelly, Costuming the Pageants, and Visiting the Cemetery. Of Poets and the 500, and Purdah in Pretoria appeared in *Dekalb Literary Arts Journal*.

The quotation from Isak Dinesen on p. 11 is reprinted by permission of Random House. The Kipling quotation on p. 31 is reprinted by permission of Mrs George Bambridge and Doubleday & Co. Inc.

Contents

STEEPLEJACKS IN BABEL

And it came to pass as they journeyed from the East that they found a plain in the land of Shinar, and they dwelt there. And they said one to another, let us make brick, and burn them thoroughly. And they had brick for stone, and slime had they for mortar. And they said, let us build a city and a tower, whose top may reach unto heaven, and let us make a name, lest we be scattered abroad upon the face of the whole earth.

GENESIS 11: 1-4

What the sirens sang

Who seals the ear sets free the eye.
No light we cannot enter by.

Green on the starboard, red to port,
The sea's directions pay you court.

They are the poles of your content;
And where you go and where you went

Divide you, who will not regain,
Unmarked, the certain course. One chain

Will rankle always on your wrist,
Along your spine be scored the mast.

Though, while you watch, the emerald
Phosphors and is a plural world,

Your former, deep and garnet, edges
Primally the wake's long wedge.

Choose: simple hearth you knew before;
Dexterous brass on a verdant shore.

All vision passes, and the choice.
Thereafter, will the wax have voice?

Advise you, 'Let the graphic fire
Draw on the wall your whole desire — '

9

Night free of envy, free of sight;
And in the mornings (shape, not light),

Your sinister, domestic fate:
Home's still warm ash that fits the grate.

BUNDLES FOR FASCISTS

And those people whom I named, Mesdames, were evil and cruel. But all the same, I shall not go back, now that those people of whom I have spoken are no longer there. Those people belonged to me, they were mine. They had been brought up and trained, with greater expense than you, my little ladies, could ever imagine or believe, to understand . . .

Isak Dinesen, BABETTE'S FEAST

The procurator is aware that palms sweat

The hands I wash, I wash advisedly.
The thief I pardon — he is freed to steal,
Theft being, by its nature, rendered thee,
And so the lesser evil. Caesar, Hail!

The vain young man who scourges, who is kissed,
Betrayed, himself is scourged, and all for youth,
May find, in dampened silver, truth I lost
In salvered water. Yes; but what is truth?

13

Manchuria 1931

Guard duty by the railhead, where the rails
Run into sand, and burlap on high bales

Is ragged in the wind. His angles steep,
The pack-train camel sleeps a shaggy sleep.

He sleeps; I yawn. I settle in my coat;
I feel the dry cold tighten in my throat.

I go on; east or west, I do not know.
Direction, absent in these sands below,

Above is blazoned in the clustered stars,
That chart us, light by light, their blue bazaars,

Their shining trade, their far-flung conquest. Dim,
Descending to the eastern, western rim,

They light, a little, parting caravans
That are their own horizon; or, intense

Among our errant locomotive sparks,
Align the several and smoking darks;

Until – an east of easts and type of types –
The rising sun stands in a sky of stripes;

And I can see, who feel it in my eyes,
A yellow sand that levels out the ties.

14

A crown for the Kingfish

(the Huey P. Long Bridge, New Orleans)

Patrol car sirens, anywhere they're bound,
Are, finally, the sine curve done in sound.

In the vicinity of this one bridge,
Though formulary, they are still cortege;

As, underneath that publicizing steel,
The river is an earth and burial:

A redneck mud that past the creole streets
Parades its plethora of old defeats.

The pomps are their reciprocal. Each guard,
Each Buick, each machine-gun late reward

The early want. Innate, it nonetheless
Is colored, channeled, by its time and place.

No empire that the hearth has not rehearsed;
No leader who was not gauleiter first.

Utilitarian, yet arrogant,
A bridge is too exact a monument.

Its profile is the bow cut down and strung.
It is the weapon chosen, challenge flung;

Is hickory turned into metal: all
The taut boy was, and now, all he will be.

Cain precedes Adam, and the central tree,
If knowledge later, first is arsenal.

15

The last of Vichy

(*Dakar*)

Dust on the harbor; high chutes coal the tramp.
The concrete villas darken in the damp,
And in the land they point to, I was born.
Alien color, be now alien corn.

One knows one's harvest. Can its site deceive?
Or will the soot, the stalagmitic, leave
Intact the live defeat, the treadmill flight,
The attitudinized pursuit. By right

My lot should be division. I am whole,
And have the whole. The parody is all.
Mansard and mosque, and tree-lined boulevards
So far from France, so near the livestock yards.

Long out of uniform, and going gray,
The Legion take the Tonkinese café.
They, irreducibly imperial,
German or blackface, always know their role.

I too have at my distance served my evil.
By it you endured. When you cavil
Bear in mind that in my brief high noon
I might have made this *Grösser Kamerun*.

Sandblasted into grandeur, pure, rebuilt,
Home may assume the profit, enjoy the guilt.
In each, there is assured support from Bonn.
I, meanwhile, live as though my side had won.

16

I note the headland through the brilliant haze;
Coffee and cocoa black and tan my days.
In the harbor that sustains one — vision, fortress,
Farce — one flies the colors of the port.

The condemned of Belgrano

(*Buenos Aires*)

Tile and turret, tin and vane
Inquire in Witch if mice are nibbling.
Male and grounded, I maintain.
Enter, Hänsel. Leave your sibling.

You may touch the pitch; no risk.
I am a host who has no ovens.
In Empress Frederick, on my desk,
Behold the patron saint of cravens.

She in weeds and I with gout
Await a tryst already over,
Having been in love with doubt
But dubious of any lover.

Bismarck was, in any case,
A fearful chaperon. The German,
Yet, is frightened of his ease,
And I of herring, work, and women.

How I have profited from tar!
No dividend whose every peso
Does not bring the Elbe; no scar,
No wound does not forbid I say so;

Whom the very cashing, there
And here, empinions, still the debtor;
Whom sharp steeples, straight in air,
Make crooked daggers in the water.

18

Distance, absence, undefile.
Take from my dark and bevelled mirrors
Asphalt that obscures them. Style,
Give back a time but take its terrors.

Split, young man, and be the seraphs
Sooty at my gate. Be one
Upon my right hand, one upon
My left ... and two to whom 'tis given –
However late – to guide my steps to Heaven.

Eva beatified

Sra. Peron's body, embalmed in 1952 'to assure abso-
lute corporeal permanence,' in 1955 was removed in
secret and buried in the River Plate.   A P

Hieratic horseflesh, marble wings,
The mighty monuments uphold in parks
Their superheroes out of comic books.
David impersonators, for whom slings
Seem reticules, they guard the patriarchs
The Jockey Club dependably erects.

Inert, they pass in strenuous review
Before one mightier, which is not there:
A mausoleum so ornate, so sheer,
Existence would betray it, as those few
Whole stories tortured Babel from its air.
It is ambition naked of its sphere.

She whom it holds, the pharaonic, nickeled
Exhibition, terminal forever
And the half-Lenin made whole, gives over
What she is to be as she is cycled.
Emptied, filling, she is still the mover —
Will the plated needles cannot sever.

Freed, her other selves attend her. They,
Thick necks made classic by the Psyche knot,
Once entered one by one their muddied fate.
The *Ewigweibliche* in gold lamé,
Ayesha trusts the flame and soon is soot;
Eve knows the canker and forgets the fruit.

Pacelli and the Ethiop

The Italian government's representations to the Vatican's secretary of state, Cardinal Eugenio Pacelli, had their effect. The Holy See did not further condemn the potential aggressor.
George W. Baer, THE COMING OF THE ITALIAN-ETHIOPIAN WAR

Unlikely angels, although by and large well met,
The pontiff and the emperor embattle yet –
Their paradise Geneva's giant Follies set.

One is a stately, beady-eyed old barracuda,
One some crypto-Coptic, bearded living Buddha.
The League of Nations hears again the Lion of Judah:

'True, I am a slaver. Now, as true confessor,
I demand the Church inculpate the aggressor.'
Whereat the Earthly Vicar, ever the recessor,

Recedes into his role as papal secretary:
'That queen whom you succeeded ... Matabele Hari ...
The fat one ... Did you give her poison, Ras Tafari?'

'What is truth?' inquires the League, and then dissolves.
The exiled emperor is forced to sell his slaves;
The pontiff washes in the silver bowl that saves.

A ballade for Mr Rhodes

(Cape Town, the Matopos, Academia, Pretoria)

THE ARCHITECT

Teak and force and whitewash, tiled and broad,
How the house subjects its client! He,
So vehement to be a myth, instead
Is in these walls the single shrill cliché:
The bluff, the inarticulate. I free,
Though he is jailed – an aging, Landseer dog
Upon an all-confining hearth. Who see
In heavy mantelpiece and dummy log
The knowing stage designer ... let the peak
My porches open on confound them; they,
And when the deep bay-windows cleave the fog,
The pacing posturer whom I obey.

THE POET

Here is the grave, and the mentality
Of added codicil, eternal flame:
The whole of Stonehenge in a chartered sky
To raise one slab with nothing save his name.
Venue of what Homeric rite, what game,
The mountain is as yet without them. Myth
Or tribute, both elude him. All the same,
They do occur. Theatrical this death,
Theatrical, elsewhere, the torches, wrath,
And massive stadia. They are at once
Themselves, and what we see: this grave and path ...
Two native warders dozing on their guns.

22

THE SCHOLARS

The final creatures of the final will,
We write the end of empire. If we fail
As athletes or as SS men, we thrill
To find that we are scholars. Not to hail,
Or seem to hail the founder, we revile
DeBeers, and take up women socially.
A little of his style informs us still.
In manner, any of us – paid the fee –
Might be his secretary. So end he,
Idea, gold, and we; they a charade
Real forever at Anzac Beach, and we,
Each year, an academic Jameson Raid.

THE MYTH

Too literal to wonder what myth is,
I have become one. Servants, misfits, you
Who serve your princes, I was raised a shepherd.
Now, an idol like a cast-iron stove,
I rule my city. Birds, I am informed,
Nest in my top hat. They are regte boere;
Let them. Lime or homage, what the harm?
Safe in the fold the undone flock, and mine
The golden fatherland, the strapping sons.

The entrance of Winifred into Valhalla

The Festspielhaus remained an object of considerable embarrass-
ment. By the terms of Siegfried Wagner's will it was the sole property
of his widow Winifred, whom a denazification court placed in 1947
in the group of major collaborators with the Nazi regime.
                    Geoffrey Skelton, WAGNER AT BAYREUTH

As if to judge, the gods survey a darkened house.
The music that has made them real will let them see.

Mystic abyss or simple pit, the orchestra
Divides and distances. They will be accurate.

Being eternal, they observe in those who watch
All who have watched here ever. Whom they now elect

Will link and will epitomize. In one reprieve
Endure the kings and Cosima, Herr Hitler, she,

And the aloof GI's. If these, unwittingly
Or well aware, make up tradition, hers alone

Is that tradition's grandeur; who, as trustees must,
Will yield or will defy, will use and cast aside;

Will make her peace with evil, take her toll of good;
And further, having once delivered up her trust,

Will live with her decisions. Not the pure blood-Wagner,
Nor the Liszt incursion, nor the sons to come

24

Outrank that force whose only name is guardian;
Toward whose intent defer at last her agents: Reich,

The godless shades of Weimar, and the gods themselves;
Who, merciless of eye and sensible of heel,

Not looking back, sets foot upon the Rainbow Bridge.

25

Leander of the diving board

(the Riefenstahl Olympia)

No Hellespont divides my goal from me.
Immobile in my narrow air, I reach,
In any given frame, the shore I seek.
The fickle Hero is the Leica eye.

Not German-Greek, I am not washed ashore.
If later I act out the tableau, weight
May then betray me; though I cross – full dress –
Dark ice soft-focused in a sniper's lens.

Blood and flatiron

Stiff in the fitted uniform
Starch as idea: for the warm,

Wet skin the warning touch of chill;
In the indifferent fabric, will.

In the façade becoming slack
It is the cool, implied rebuke.

Starch is how vanity, how care
Have made the shirt a shirt of hair,

And on the dripping, tropic site
Create the drillground anchorite —

Himself that shaft he occupies,
And he as desert of its rise.

Chevrons or stigmata, the signs
Embellish only. Discipline

Is under, in the stubborn shape
That forms the cross or fights the nape;

That, neither line nor meaning, means
The more. Its message: how to seem.

It sketches, on the body's tense
Attention, rest without suspense.

27

The faint, defiant show of ease
It answers with a knife-edge crease:

There on the flesh its outlines smother,
The hard and vegetable other.

Carpenters

Forgiven, unforgiven, they who drive the nails
    Know what they do: they hammer.
  If they doubt, if their vocation fails,
    They only swell the number,

Large already, of the mutineers and thieves.
    With only chance and duty
  There to cloak them, they elect and nail.
    The vinegar will pity.

Judas who sops, their silver his accuser, errs
    To blame the unrewarded.
  They guard the branch he hangs from. Guilt occurs
    Where it can be afforded.

29

THE THOUGHTFUL ISLANDS
AND THE JUST REPUBLICS

God bless the thoughtful islands,
*   Where never warrants come,*
God bless the just republics
*   That give a man a home.*

Rudyard Kipling

Purdah in Pretoria

The corrugated iron vibrates in thunder;
On the covered sidewalk, sun. Far under,
Gallon cans of bloom, and I the vendor.

Matronly, no lissome violet seller,
I ornament an air forever stiller:
I the turbulence and I the color.

Group unproven, area obscure,
Eviction certain. This is how I parry:
Caste mark, lipstick, corset, sari.

Blue, the jacarandas by my corner
Tangle in the lightning. On the burner,
Sidewalk curry draws the true discerner.

Old friends still are best. I once was svelte,
He the Vice Squad in a Sam Browne belt.
Hale and red and Dutch Reformer, well

Toward middle age, in shade already gusty
He precedes the hail.
                    The alley's dusty,
So I indicate my door. 'Tea, Rusty?'

Two hymns

I

THE AFRIKANERS IN THE ARGENTINE
(1902)

You bring us, Lord, from all our loss
To useless hope, beside a second veldt.
Remove and fixative the seas we cross;
No land but home the image held.

The spacious grass, stiff under frost,
Is there as here a planet white on gold.
Such fields, such level sweeps as we have lost,
If space were all, space still might hold.

River nor pampa, silver, mud,
Can now return us, in their tongue of Spain,
The earth-and-silver of the tongue now slain.
And though, raised of our pillared blood,

Arise again the strong, plain church,
It, too, must be a wife to Lot. Look back,
Look forward, there the plain, the cities. Watch:
In static grain, now ends the trek.

II

CONFEDERATES IN BRAZIL
(1866)

Unreconstructed, uncontrite,
We seek the land that we have known by night.
The state of day we can endure to lose.
Never the dark of ancient use.

So long as, on the latticed vine,
The torrid moonlight seeps its gold and brine,
And in the garden pools the flashing carp
Give back its colors, but more sharp,

In that wet tension, haze on water,
Hang yet the motes cast out as of no matter:
Indulgence, common forms, observance, ease;
And, suspended even as these,

Their last illusion: continuity.
Sustain, night, still the same, still other,
Haze and past. By thy filled eye
Make one the mote and beam, the slave and brother.

35

DeLesseps go home

(Culebra, 1889)

The drunk Jamaicans cease to ditch, and I,
In fever, lay the unreal tripod by.

Surveyor, contract labor, we alike
Learn by delirium to yield the dike

That we are not the Dutch Boys of. Be brave,
And any stock exchange will dig your grave.

Far ticker tape and white liana, bell
Or sky of glass, what have you made us sell

That we should see, as if we fired them still,
Cold engines of the serpent's cloven hill?

Hospital, need I say, goes on: brass bed,
Enamel bedpan, nun with leaden tread.

Have you in Picardy, *Ma Soeur, Ma Chère*,
A world whose savings are invested here?

Say to them: on the mole at Port Said
Their idol stands who fails us in our need;

Who, though he once built there on sand, displays
Here that clay will be his feet of clay;

That green and sugared hope burns off as dunder;
That it will not be we who put asunder.

Tripod and fever, Mother Combat Boots,
Qualify the prophet. By his fruits

You know him; by the dirt-trains whose each car
Is painted USA, or UAR;

That seem this rust we see, but that will haul,
Piecemeal, the toppled idol off the mole.

New vine-shoots fill the firebox edge to edge;
Fresh-water fishes repossess the dredge.

Vultures over Ancon Hill

(Balboa, C.Z.)

Staircase and flag, in single ladder,
Band the sky. By fiat sadder

For their dream of marble halls,
The Zone proconsuls set the tolls.

Below their hill, Balboa High
Embalms the years that pass it by.

Blameless haircuts, sweaters fitted,
Who Would Be, if the heat permitted,

Cheerleaders, are, for lack of state,
Old territorials. A late

Too little, they confront Lenin
With only Tom Swift's time machine.

None, as an older dreadful says,
'Surmise,' but neither did Cortez,

Not being present. In their ken
Swims Theodore's own Darien:

The curving bay, its opal calms,
Viceregal streets of royal palms;

And there above, the columned height.
Is it McKim, or Mead, or White?

38

Cerro Ancon, above your slopes
Is helix of the bird who hopes.

An oldest bolshevik, time's true adherent
Maximizes death on every current.

Gauchesco

The dying cattle stumble from the mallet,
Who, however, stumbled toward it. He,
Their late conductor, spreads his shawl for pallet
To lie down by the chinaberry tree.

Fermenting berries move by on the blood;
Four chickens peck and swallow. Merry eyes
And bloody apron, blood upon his cards,
The old man deals a solitaire and plays.

The game comes out; the cows queue up and bellow.
Lighting charcoal in a punctured drum,
He waits. The waiting beef is thick with tallow;
The chickens have red bosoms and are drunk.

Plot for a Guianese operetta

The Dual Monarchy, despite its unique understanding of the problems involved in the co-existence of various languages and races, at the present time desires no African or Asian colonies. Count Berchtold

Baroque of steeple, tropical of width and air,
St. Florian among the Heathen fronts the square.

Street signs in German, Magyar on the obverse side,
Direct one toward the *Oper*. There, *The Bartered Bride*.

Applauding still – all standees, although no less regal –
Palm trees seem in silhouette the double eagle.

Thick though K.u.K. may monogram the lights,
The natives and the Croats strike for language rights.

Elisabeth the Kaiserin, *très décolletée,*
Uplifts a cast iron bosom toward the pigeons. They,

The nihilism in the air, lay on the heart
Their gray, corrosive chemistry.
                                        By law apart

In their Imperial and Royal new locations,
Tribal types and local Jews outline new nations.

After, when the *Prison of the Peoples* waltz
Suborns the B. Juarez Shebeen, the new wave halts.

41

Analysis each noon by cable from Vienna.
Freud is much the same. He is no better. Then a

Second, even more electric message comes:
'Archduke assassinated.' Tom-tom Boy, the drums;

We have a power failure. In the beat between,
Those outlines have an anthem. Yet the nations seen,

The drumbeat heard, are all that fill them. Man and Boy,
We have no picture save the puzzle we destroy.

In our fashion, Francis Joseph, we are *kaisertreu*.

The Shropshire Lad in Limehouse

From Wapping Stairs to Limehouse Reach,
Warehouses rise six stories each;
And if their pilings, where I boat,
At low tide smell of creosote,

On the street side, they and their cables
Are London's Hanseatic gables;
And toward that sign of Aryan blood
I forge on through the tidal mud.

My manly form, my yellow hair,
My rower's torso partly bare,
Will bring to St. Anne's Limehouse steeple
Tonio Kröger's blue-eyed people.

From Pennyfields to Wapping High
I cross the road and pass on by.
The public school that tames the beast
Brings out the Levite, or the priest;

And though I am not of the breed
That leaves a man and lets him bleed,
The chink, the wog, the frog, the toad,
Have put themselves outside the code.

Still porting on my head my scull,
I met a dialectic trull.
And while I could not quite determine,
I rather think that she was German;

For, when the viaducts shut tight
Their early colonnade of night,
And later, when each light is red,
I quite remember what she said:

Denn die einen sind im Dunkeln,
Und die andern sind im Licht,
Und man siehet die im Lichte,
Die im Dunkeln sieht man nicht.

Tonio in Mogador

In the 14th century the city of Lübeck tried unsuccessfully to found a colony in Morocco.

ENCYCLOPAEDIA BRITANNICA

'The Arabs, Lisabeta, shed their shoes;
The Lutherans lift up chorales.' So, ruse

Or accidental parallel, the spire
Invites toward Mecca, as, in gothic choir,

Do minarets toward Lübeck. Name and house,
Thin pennants of the Hansa flag the dhows,

Announcing, through the surf and toward the souks,
A merchant navy of the Buddenbrooks.

House flags triangular and sails lateen,
Those ships, each year, backdrop one scene.

Contained and blond, unknowable, surmise,
The naked surfers pose with hooded eyes.

They are the alien the veiled are not;
Who, burgherly and open, somewhat squat,

Behind their veils uncover in their glances
Damp, duple, never-ending belly dances.

Still and motion, flesh and eye, have done!
I have for home a knowledge never one:

45

The various, the twice-divided land —
Time's rich concession.
                                    See, disputed strand,

Your halves his fever and his gaze libido,
Venetian Janus on your Moorish Lido.

In Sydney by the bridge

Cruise ships are, for the young, all that which varies.
The aged disembark with dysenteries.
Always, it is middle age that sees the ferries.

They hold no promise. Forward or reverse
Impels them only to where what occurs,
Occurs. Such is, at least, the chance of being terse,

And is their grace. The lengthy liners, fraught
Sublimely, shrill for tugs. If they're distraught,
That is because the thoughts of youth are long, long thoughts –

Save those of gratitude. The slow, massed force
That frees them they will cast off in due course,
To learn, or not to learn, the ferries' sole resource:

How, in the crowding narrows, when the current
Runs in opposition and the torrent
Claws the wheel, to locate in routine, abhorrent

For the storm, the shore that makes it specious;
Where one calls the vicious, curtly, vicious,
And the scheduled ferry, not the cruise ship, precious.

By the waters of Lexington Avenue

In place of a world there is a CITY, *a* POINT.
Oswald Spengler

Their rivet guns the noise of lily gilding,
Steeplejacks top out the Chrysler Building,
Which is height, and the idea height.
Tongue unconfused and the begun complete,

It will evoke us still that pride which beckons
And the sky it arrogates; that tokens,
On the equal plain, all enterprise
And all distinction. In its rise

Diminish sun-dried brick, harp, worker, river.
Held in that bright steel, there shine, forever,
Grounded lightning and the closing storm,
The ticker tape and the cuneiform.

Now, exile, when the rivets cool in silence
And the hot sky waits, two forces balance:
Derrick, and the pinnacle it lifts.
The summit locks in place; the concrete shafts

Anticipate the elevator cables.
Neither harp nor pendulum, their able,
Twanging sound must yet pursue you; home
The exile, time the long captivity they strum.

But for that little while the shafts stay silent,
And at their climax, jerking, brilliant,
Lightning waits for thunder, will to power
Then conquers the quotidian. Pure tower

Stands. Let the reach and moment stand for all:
These tethered skies, and space through which they fall;
New conquests, age, the music it debars;
A Wall Street lunar skyline, Shinar, Mars.

L'aigle a deux jambes

(*on a photograph of Sarah Bernhardt in* L'AIGLON)

Eagle into swayback Ganymede,
The predator and prey become one breed;

Crippling Time the only Metternich,
Ego the only cup. As pallid duke,

For all the jack boots and the ducal sash,
You still are the devouring mother – ash

The taste, compulsive the desire. If Jove
Had finally his nectar, what you have

Is this: bankruptcy, fright wig, and a limp.
But while you've alexandrine for your pimp

You ravish; cruel in the knowledge that,
Olympian at last, you serve your fate;

Intransigence your courage, myth your art.
A rarer bird, a truer Bonaparte,

Across the steppes of your decay – in drag –
You stump toward Moscow on a wooden leg.

50

Off the freeway

The all night station, vertical as noon,
To all that shades returns the shadow. Moon

And planet, other moons, above the pumps
The lettered globes shine on the garbage dumps,

To make of No-Knock and of New Lead-Free
Their Ptolemaic, fixed astronomy.

Born to the signs and system closed, the neo-
Magus trapped here would, if Galileo

Rose again to threaten now his franchise,
Cry 'Lynch the socialist' to save the ranch house.

It is not paid for, but one has for hope
The closing stock quotes, crosswords, horoscope.

One dozes, letting fall the loan shark's pencil.
Outside, wind chimes the advertising tinsel.

The vended foods are going brightly rotten;
Two empty pumps seem *Frauen ohne Schatten.*

In the dreams of enterprise still free
No bell for service sounds, no horns decree.

And what one does not see need never mock –
This past, this present, where one does not look:

The turning tinsel, brilliantly awake;
The young attendant, frankly on the make.

Of poets and the 500

Come back to Indiana — not too late!
                    Hart Crane

Man overboard, and one presumes
In so impersonal a tomb

Some chic new current still is Hart.
A motion only, part and not part

Of what should be his element,
Once more he fails of his intent.

No epic heat, no turn of phrase
His submarine sidewalk cafes

Do not hallucinate. If seas
Have surer cities, they are these:

The solid towns that tax and tithe,
Whose prairie streets still show the scythe.

Enduring, elemental *urbs*,
The Duesenberg adorns your curbs.

Continuing city, sure style, years
Seamless as Greek hexameters

Connect your pleasure, pace your poise.
In their respective walls of noise,

Hart thunders toward his wordy quagmire,
Achilles toward the checkered flag.

The prisoners' variety

Inept and earnest, in a style arrears,
The one performance spans how many years?

Forever far from any talent scout,
It is *The Time Machine* the men act out.

In these impersonations (by the lifers)
Runs a code their middle age deciphers,

Saying, 'This is where we each came in.'
Kay Kyser, Russ Colombo live again;

And though the lyrics seem release enough,
It is not love these are the prisoners of.

Iron-Jaw Bennett scrapes his steel guitar;
Miss Diane is where the actions are.

The talent is to grind and bump, or scrape;
The genius was murder, theft, or rape.

So, Custom, they have nothing to declare ...
Depression here, and affluence out there.

If Beauty waken, can the kiss of greed
Update the sleeping wood? Or, too late freed,

Do fey Diane and what Prince Charming, torn
From context, bleed once more on Time's sure thorn:

Their wound release, their torture, its refinement.
The only stanching – sleep – is reconfinement.

Drinking song for tired jaycees

For Janet Lewis at the Red Dog Saloon

A cagey sibyl, kitsch, a red plush cavern.
Far from students need a far from tavern.

Sibylline with a difference, too shrewd
By far to let the future here intrude,

You rather, when you belt it, foretell backward.
Baby grand your tripod, and the awkward

Fact of old age well obscured, you tell
Present tense the past will yet be well:

That senior members caught in junior chambers
Yet will know, sharp in that damp November,

The huddled players linked by muddy hands,
The cardboard placards in the windy stands;

That on the blackballed and select together
Now must fall, late though it see them gather,

Some echo of the stein and sabre cut;
Debased however, of a style they state.

Boys – though you be drummer, college, gay, or mama's –
Here is an all-inclusive *Gaudeamus*.

54

For you who drink now, blade will yet re-echo,
Visored cap fit still the rambling wreck.

It is a form, if not of feeling steady,
Then of feeling whole.
                                    Janet, vamp till ready.

The dispositions of retirement pay

Late naps, loose ends. The twenty year enlistment up;
The good life it prepared still tentative as sleep.

Gin, orange juice. The sunny condominium,
Paid fully, now is trophy, now the trophy room.

Jet lacquer out of Hong Kong, teak, authentic brass.
New Guinea and the Marshalls, Indo-China twice;

And if they loom always, or if they quite recede,
The form they gave continues: ease, but as the need

Demands, the small-scale talent given honestly.
Ease, what will the demand hereafter be? To say,

Of any idle love, it challenges? Or, once
The challenge has evaporated, to renounce

Each as a blackmail: one more trip-wire in the hurried,
Shallow side-world where the patently unmarried

Form a jungle on their own. Part of the time
A part time job will partly fill. If, wholly grim,

It will not call the whole man forth again, it may,
In pity, dull the knowledge he is far away,

Still planning, in whatever jungle end is means.
All is as planned, yet somehow cheat. The razor hums;

The paper and the morning lie outside the door.
The inexperienced young man is forty-four.

Where the cross is made

(*Papeete*)

The perfect schooner bobs at anchor, ease
Uneasy on the perfect bay. Masts stark
And rigging bare, among the random stars
Exactly move her restless diagrams.

Eternal light and fickle hemp, idea
Beckoned out of heaven by device,
The moment's constellations come and go:
Orion never, briefly Dippers, Cross

More often. Cruciform and variants,
Night's single vision wrung, in fast, in blood,
Of useless sands and vasty idleness,
Utility can rig on any mast.

Terry meets the Lusiads

The low bronze lions lord their English bank,
Succinct Gibraltars of the Hong Kong trading floor:
    The symbol noble but the feline rank,
    As if the perfidies were there, and stank.

Low temples, on the Macaense shore,
Have for their symbol Fortune in a grosser guise.
    Gautama or the new casino – whore –
    It is the Wheel of Things they bow before:

Our giddy empress. Lifting rheumy eyes,
The Buddha, over double chin, cries faites vos jeux.
    The bony croupier, serene, all-wise,
    Draws profit from the path he must advise.

The wheel releases whom its slots prefer.
And on the Hong Kong bourse the bank shares fluctuate;
    They ticker-tape an Albion less sure,
    But more perfidious. It will endure,

At least as Portugal endures. The state
That is the withering away of state, the city
    Uncontinuing, alike await,
    Last chips not yet in place, the turn of Fate.

MAPPING THE LOST CONTINENT

In the land of great aunts

I
MAKING BLACKBERRY JELLY

In gallon cans, the berries fill the kitchen:
One of red to eight of ripe. Escutcheon,

Challenge of the wholly confident,
Her labels—dated, as if vintage meant—

Already mark the glasses. Never once
The aid of Sure-Jell, 'never once one ounce

To turn to sugar.' White, the cotton sacks
Await that purple they will strain. Attacks

(Appendicitis) come from eating seeds,
And jam does not quite suit the artist's needs:

The primal urge to seal in paraffin
Some essence wholly clarified. Thick, thin,

Remain the juices all which they have been.
The loose white blossom on the pale green vine;

These tiny chandeliers as dark as wine.
Clustering seed-pearls turned to red, the time

Of ripeness, and the other time of dread—
The liquid flood of birth; its jelling dead.

Pour out the total, for the rest is chance;
Pectin will shape now, or ferment advance.

Seal! Tyrian purple is from cotton wrung;
The whole of sense is gathered on the tongue.

II
COSTUMING THE PAGEANT

The neat fire falters in the polished grate;
The treadle, oiled and mute, fails at such rate

As daylight and the ankle fail. Stout seamstress,
Is the robe you sew your one remonstrance –

Satin, tinsel – for this winter room
And year round solitude? Or in that tome

(The Doré Bible) open on your Singer
Is the pattern all: a wire coat-hanger

Bent for halo, cheesecloth cut for wings.
And if each host that with the angel sings

May also be, aloft in close formation,
Lucifer and cohorts, age and gumption

Are the lance to keep him still at bay.
Now, on her fingers – late – community

Has marked its own. Tenacious brass, the tinsel
Stains. Out of season, not the cup and chancel,

Yet communion all the same. She takes,
Receiver, giver of the gift she makes:

A gold, a frankincense of usefulness,
And myrrh of old achievement, strong to bless.

The practiced poker will command the embers;
Out of the treadle will the angel come.

III
VISITING THE CEMETERY

Who of these ordered dead, the named and grouped,
Has lost particularity? Descript,

If curtly, dated by the mason's art,
They form a whole of which she knows each part:

A branching genealogy in stone.
The stone tree flowers; the lineal, made one

In floral line with the collateral,
Have each the bloom her yard-man puts on all –

The eighteen small glass jars, as many flowers.
Upright, the yard-man stoops. His mistress towers.

Afternoon is quiet, and is not;
As if the dead were so much unforgot

They had a far, familiar pulse. Again,
Again, the sawmill sounds and is the kin.

If, when the Negro tends her grave as well
(It being somehow tacit that he will);

If her stone means to no one, least to him,
Well-being and the warm continuum,

Do these consanguine join the non-descript?
The lumber says deny, the shade accept.

Between, the dead are what they were. For what they are,
The early jonquil glistens in the mason jar.

Dubieties

Into the wound the living hand;
There, underneath the unstilled heart,
To ease the doubt. The stillness spanned,

Hiatus of the pulse apart
And trust returning in the beat,
Shall I uncover (doubt my art)

Suspicion in its very heat?
Of thorn, of lance and sponge and chill,
Suspect this rhythm does not treat.

Doubt you, as you would doubt as well
That in the sub-divided bread
The wheat might still be actual,

That of the one still of the dead
The heart's partitioned off-beat tells.
And if the hand I bring back red

Has learned alone that where it spills
Or where it drums, the blood, like rain,
Can bear no message, have its skills

Trust only one another; vein
Go darker, artery stay bright;
Be death decipherable to sight.

65

Professionals

Itinerant astrologers of no great wealth,
We leave three gifts as winning teams might drink a health;
The whole point being, not the goal, however termed,
But how our distant calculation stands confirmed.

Our bright conjunction splits to its component stars;
We part. Dark Heaven, give again your text we parse,
That, by the well-loved exercise, the known arcane,
We keep our pride. If, through arcana not our own,

We still may end as fable, need true cameleers
Seem quack familiars? Substance of the gold, the years,
Become ourselves that which we are in other eyes:
Three kings of Orient, by reputation wise.

Cartography is an inexact science

The known world ends, and of the map's vague monsters
    We are one:
   A beast to fill in blanks.
  Not limits, but the limits passed,

We thrive a little, one the other's climate,
    Our two backs
   A sort of landfall. Drift,
  For all who come there, almost warms.

Behind us in those bordered lands, does custom,
    Growing old,
   Map still? Must all who love,
  In time, elaborate this unknown edge?

*This book was printed at the press of David R. Godine
in Brookline, Massachusetts. The design is by Carol Shloss.
The text was set in Monotype Perpetua
by Wolf Composition Company,
printed on a specially made Almanac Text,
and bound by A. Horowitz & Son.*